*These ruins I have shored against
my fragments.*

CONTENTS

SHORT STORIES

the minister	*page* 9
party	18
so what do you think about gaza?	24

POEMS

the wall	29
windrush elegy	30
abdul kareem	31
looksmaxxing	32
tourists	33
mortality	34
sundays	35
waiting tables	36
apparuit	37
traffic	38
break-up	39
grasmere	40
stood up	41
liberation	42
politics	43
tren	44
epigrams	45-56

SHORT STORIES

the minister

Couched in his deeply ergonomic chair, the minister watched the civil servants and sweating Fast Streamers file into their respective cubicles.

'Most of them get the Tube I suppose,' he said to himself. 'When was the last time I got the Tube? Must've been back in the Cameron years before I got my car. Much nicer the car. Shaded windows and everything. Of course I wouldn't have it unless I absolutely needed it, but it's a hybrid so I don't really have to care about emissions anyway. Great air conditioning too, not as good as in here but still pretty good. Colin looks pretty shabby today. I wonder what we're doing today.'

The minister swivelled in his seat for a bit, then spent twenty minutes examining the posters pinned to the wall. They had been put together rather hastily for the upcoming general election.

'BACK GUPTA,' read one, alongside a picture of the Prime Minister beaming beneath his turban; 'THE PARTY FOR GETTING AHEAD' read another, in bold type above a remote worker in an immaculately folded niqab. The last one was his favourite. The words 'FAMILY VALUES' were printed in massive letters above a brown boy standing on the White Cliffs of Dover. In the distance his large family waved to him from the prow of a Coastguard patrol boat. The versions in Arabic and Hindi were even more impressive.

'God those are clever. I mean really clever. It's about time we got the communities on side. If only the interns like Colin showed the same get-up-and-go as that girl in the café or that boy's family. When I was his age I worked twice as hard and didn't look half as shabby, and I had to commute all the way from north Islington! Now look at me, Minister for *Migration and Welcome*.'

Migration and Welcome. The words brought a massive smile to his face. So what if Mustafa had gotten Home Sec and Hassan was Defence? Those posts were old news! He was the one who would clear the way for the next generation; he was the one who would stamp the visas and build the reception centres. Nobody in their right mind could call him 'pale and stale' now! His commitment to social justice was cast iron, his devotion to a diverse Britain absolutely bona fide, and he took great pride in the historic importance of his office. He sipped his cappuccino with relish, then called up his secretary Aisha for the day's schedule.

First there was the situation in Cornwall, where unsanitary conditions in twelve of the new camps had led to a number of hospitalisations. It was agreed that he would go to the PM ASAP and see about fast-tracking the Housing for Heroes scheme. A brilliant piece of work, whereby residents in the surrounding villages would pay a fixed penalty if they refused to take in as many migrants as their homes could accommodate. Of course there would be grumbling, but he was sure that they would be more than willing to do their bit when the benefits of taking in such hard working young people were explained to them.

'If only I could take some myself, I'm sure they'd love the cottage in St. Ives, and those Gambians in *The Guardian* the other day looked splendid, simply splendid! Every one of them strong and smiling and raring to get ahead. But I can hardly be expected to fulfil my duties with just the house in the Cotswolds. Some day perhaps. Maybe when I'm in the Lords.'

Another cappuccino and another meeting, this time on the lack of refugees in the Royal Air Force. Kehinde, his favourite intern, was very enthusiastic about increasing the number of asylum seekers going to flight school.

'Ma cousin beem wantin to be pilot for years, buh dey say he can' do it cos he no have mass or science. Dey tell 'im an now he beem charged wit assault but he din' do nothin sah. Dey proper wastemen sah.'

'Your poor cousin! I'm sure we can do something about that. You're quite right that it's unfair, expecting new pilots to have such antiquated qualifications, and it's only natural that he lost his temper. A really good point Kehinde. I'll get in touch with Hassan first thing tomorrow and we'll see what we can do.'

'But sir,' interjected Colin, whose sparse blond hair was a source of irritation to the minister, 'surely the pilots need at least a little bit of maths and science? Just a little! I mean, the flight schools wouldn't just ask for them for no reason, would they?'

The minister gripped his paper cup.

'Now Colin, we've talked about this. You can't expect to understand these issues until you've worked in these communities for a long time. The youth are clamouring to fly fighter jets, simply clamouring, and who are we to tell them no just because they've not got the "proper qualifications"? Isn't that right Kehinde?'

'Das right sah.'

The minister leaned back in his chair, his free hand held out in an open gesture to show the interns he was on their level. A trick he'd picked up in the Sunak days.

'Just try and broaden your perspective Colin, that's all I'm saying yeah? Nobody here's angry, we're just trying to get you to understand that not everyone's had the opportunities you've enjoyed, and we need to make sure that everyone can get ahead together. I know it must be hard for you coming from such a privileged background-'

'-But I grew up on a council estate!'

'Well that hardly matters. What I'm trying to say is-'

'-Then an orphanage!'

'That's it! I've told you I won't have it. You could've grown up in a deep fat fryer for all I care. The fact is you've got privilege and you need to accept that, all of the studies have shown that. Frankly you're lucky to be here at all, and if it wasn't for your work on halal school meals I think I'd start to question your motives. Now why don't you get me another cappuccino while I hash this thing out with Kehinde and the others?'

With a sigh, Colin assented and shuffled off in the direction of the cafeteria. Kehinde smiled a ginormous smile and put his Balenciagas on the desk. They spent another thirty minutes on the flight schools, then considered the problem of transphobia in the Traveller community; Panorama had just released an exposé on a group outside Newcastle that had refused to lease one of their caravans to a local polycule. Technically this was the business of the Secretary for Hope not Hate, but the minister's name had been dropped a couple of times and there were rumours that Kuenssberg was gunning for him.

Eventually the clock struck three which meant it was time to go home. The minister donned his gillet and rucksack and headed for his parking space, but on the way he saw the balding civil servants and sweating interns pull out their headphones and Oyster cards, and a mad idea struck him: what if he took the Tube like he used to, all the way to his flat in Camden? What if he forgot for one day that he did probably the most important job in the country?

'Yes! No better way to show that I care, that I have a stake in this city as much as anyone. I might even get my picture in *The Independent*. Let's see what old Kuenssberg thinks about that!'

Giddy with the brilliance of his new idea he almost skipped to his ministerial parking space. He leaned over the Range Rover and waited for the window to come down. A pair of beady eyes looked up at him.

'Hi Nguyen! Hope you've had a great day. I just wanted to let you know that I've decided to take the Tube today so you can head right home.'

The beady eyes widened.

'But sir,' said Nguyen his driver, 'is *very* dangerous sir, no safe, you understand? You safe take car stay safe sir yes? Outside very dangerous.'

'No it's quite alright, really! I'll see you first thing tomorrow, eleven o'clock as always. There's really no need to worry. Goodbye!'

And with that he was off. He could tell he had really impressed Nguyen, and exited the police barricades puffed up with pride. He was so happy he didn't notice the shouts of the officer manning the machine gun, nor did he mind stepping over all the sleeping bags and threading through the tents. That being said, he still had wits enough only to tap the contactless pads of the brown vagrants. The white ones had help enough after all.

'Were there always so many tents here?' he thought to himself. 'I guess there must've been. There's no way things could've gotten worse with GDP going up like it has. But what on *earth* is that smell? My goodness it's hot.'

The walk took him around twenty minutes, hassled as he was by a great many panhandlers, but eventually he made it to Charing Cross and the Northern line. The white tiles and advertisements were almost entirely covered with graffiti, and the flaming trashcans seemed unnecessary considering the heat, but he was glad to see the Party's posters. They had been put up yesterday or the day before, and one could still make out parts of the design beneath the painted genitalia and gang signs. He looked up at the one working display.

DELAYZ: TRAIN COME SOON NORTHERN HIGH BARNET. PLEASE DO NEEDFUL WAIT. NO STAND ON LINE PLEASE VERY GOOD.

'Well! That's a bit annoying. But I'm sure it won't be long, and it's good to see they've made the display text more accessible.'

The minister was really sweating now. Just as he took off his gillet and stuffed it into his rucksack, a high pitched scream announced the train. Sparks flew in the gloom of the tunnel as it approached and the crowd surged forward. He was pushed into the car so violently he didn't notice the people on the tracks or the commuters clinging to the roof. Nevertheless, something did seem really odd to him about all this. He'd have to get in touch with Bytyqi the Transport Secretary and ask him about the Northern line. In any case, he was sure the others would be working like they used to; otherwise, what had Bytyqi and his ministers done with the three billion they'd been given by the Tube Improvement bill?

It took him a whole hour to get to Camden on account of 'blockages' on the line, and he chided himself for forgetting his San Pellegrino. He had to settle for a warm bottle of Buxton offered him by a pedlar. Just before he arrived at his stop, an altercation of some sort took place in the adjoining car. The screams were terribly loud, so loud that they could be heard over the screeching of the train's brakes, and the minister wondered what on earth could be the cause of such commotion. When he was shunted out on to the platform he looked to his right for the source of the agitation, and saw two enormous, vascular dogs, that mauled their way past the crowd of commuters and skittered up the stairs; Guatemalan Giga Bullies, a breed unfortunately omitted from the latest Dangerous Dogs Act.

The lifts and the escalators were out so he trudged up the stairs. When finally he reached the exit around 5 o'clock his shirt was soaked through and he was quite fatigued. What's more, the discussion of transphobic Gypsies had gone on for so long that he'd missed lunch. After showing his ID to the officer guarding the turnstyles, he headed off in search of nourishment. He didn't have to go very far - the entire high street had been transformed into a sort of bazaar - and soon snapped up a couple of pakoras and a cold chai latte. He sat down beside some Bangladeshis busy kneading dough with their feet, and enjoyed his hard-earned repast.

'This is stupendous! Of course it's a little wet and oily, and the meat could stand to have less hair on it, but overall you can't complain, certainly not for forty pounds!'

A vague cloud of spice exploded from a nearby stall. He coughed violently between sips of his latte.

'Cinnamon? Yes definitely some cinnamon, and some other stuff as well. Much better than stuffy roasted chestnuts or, God forbid, exhaust fumes! With a little luck the entire city'll soon be pedestrianised. After all, how could anyone want to drive past this? Think of all the culture they'd be missing.'

The Bangladeshis were stamping on the dough with furious intensity now, in time to the insane tune of a nearby pungi. His coughing became extremely violent; his hair stuck to his forehead and his whole body heaved, until he saw a drop of blood land on the greasy remains of his pakora.

'Oh my. That can't be good. I've not had a nosebleed like this since my trip to Bali in second year. Maybe there was something in the cappuccino? Damn that Colin! God I feel awful, I feel tired, I need my San Pellegrino…'

The minister fell from his plastic crate and went into convulsions on the floor, desperately clutching his pakora. A crowd gathered around him, a sea of brown faces which showed absolutely no regard for his plight. He jabbered to himself feverishly.

'God look the community's here isn't that something. Real solidarity, coming together at last to get ahead for a better Britain my God. The blood is hot on my nose was hot in Bali too I hope they call an ambulance I think I can make it only forty minutes if they call now. What is that feeling tugging on my wrist oh, it's a boy taking my watch. Well good I didn't need that watch he's probably going to take it and go to school or set up a business God, look at me, even now helping the next generation. Entrepreneurship getting ahead graft grit my God. Is it getting dark so early on a day like this so early? Getting dark in the communities… My God.'

The minister's eyes rolled over. He gave one final heave, and was still. Another child soon started working on his shoes. A fight broke out over his rucksack and gillet. His latte was enjoyed by an overheating mongrel. An hour or so went by until a police armoured vehicle found him. By then he'd been stripped to his underwear and a pigeon had defecated on his forehead.

His funeral was an elaborate affair, considering the fact that most people had been banned under Net Zero laws from anything save the most threadbare services. Eulogies were pronounced by other members of the government. Prime Minister Gupta smiled and spoke of his 'very nice levelling up for all of us.' Bytyqi, Hassan and Mustafa echoed his sentiments. But the most touching tribute of all came from Kehinde, who had been invited to speak by the minister's wife (they were very close; he had even been to visit her in St. Ives.)

'Dah ministah was always goodman to me. He no care I no have mass and science. But I know he wan' me to say dat we still got to make it so dat nobody been held back by no havin them, like my cousin who didn't do nuffin an now he's being charged. I want to thank ministah big lady too; she get me nice shoes and tings.'

As you can imagine, there wasn't a dry eye in the house after such a powerful speech, and the waves of sobbing drowned out the sound of the water cremation.

. . .

A few months later Colin took a trip to the Lake District with some friends from work. They had to avoid the nicer parts, which were now reserved BIPOC spaces, but they still managed to find a suitably picturesque path through the hills. Eventually they ascended so far that the calls to prayer grew faint, and Colin let himself relax. The wind felt good in his sparse blonde hair, and the dumpy girl from the Department of Hope not Hate made suggestive glances in his direction. Just as he edged closer to her, a droning sound came out of the clouds above. Colin craned his neck skyward just in time to see the F-35 hurtling down towards him. A second later there was a stupendous explosion and Colin was flung into a nearby tree. He had recovered his senses just enough to look around for his friends, when suddenly something fell, smoking, into his lap. To his horror he saw that it was a leg. A black leg in a black flight suit, with a large and crispy Balenciaga trainer on the foot.

'Maths and science,' he whispered to himself, between spurts of blood, 'just a little bit of maths and science...'

party

'Hey! Having fun?'

'Yeah it's great, thanks. So, what do you study?'

'I do IR.'

'Oh. What year?'

'Third year now.'

Third year? So he's what, twenty, twenty-one? How on earth is he so bald? If that happened to me I'd go on a rampage, drive a truck into a supermarket or something.

'So getting real now I guess?'

'Yeah I guess so. Working on the diss takes up most of my time.'

'I'll bet.'

Jesus. Just look at this place. And no roommates! Must be at least two thousand a month. I wonder how he pays for it? Mummy and daddy of course. Should I ask? Better not.

'Well, thanks for having me. It's a great party.'

'Hey no problem! Thanks for coming.'

I need a cigarette. Guess I can't smoke in here, mummy and daddy wouldn't allow it. There's a garden downstairs though I think.

'Excuse me,

Coming through!

Just going for a smoke sorry.'

Look how worn the steps are! This place must be at least two hundred years old. Bloody dark as well you'd think they could keep on the lights, careful not to slip you've had a few already. Which door? Back door obviously. Come on you piece of shit open up. There we go. Fuck me it's cold I should have brought my coat. People out here already? Great.

'Hi! Anyone got a light?'

'Sure thing here.'

'Thanks.'

Building's much uglier on this side. Air conditioners and brickwork. Garden's like a prison yard or something with all those lights coming down, I really wish they'd dim the lights. And the music is dreadful. Whoever's on the aux should be shot.

'So what do you do dude?'

Oh for fuck's sake.

'Me? History.'

'Oh sick that's cool man. Bet it's tough to find work though.'

'Right.'

'I do business.'

'I see.'

I wish this prick would leave me alone. What is he smoking anyway? Jesus. It's a blunt. Who brings a blunt? He'll be out here all night with his hangers-on. Who's that at the window? It's him. Somehow he looks even balder, must be the wind. He must hate it. Wait a minute, who is he talking to? Fucking hell, it's Amy. He's actually trying it on with Amy. I suppose he is pretty tall...

'Yo you want a hit man?'

'No, thank you.'

If he ends up with Amy I'll top myself. What the fuck does she see in him? Apart from the money of course. Jesus, she's smiling. What did he say he studied? IR I think. I bet he's talking about Burundi, girls love it when you talk about Burundi. UN peacekeeping and 'problems in the region.' How does he always look so self-assured? What's his secret? I need a piss. Can't take one out here.

'Heading back inside man?'

'Yes.'

'Alright dude stay chill man.'

These fucking people. Alright, take a piss, then get another drink and mill about for a bit. See if they're still talking and if she's likely to stay the night. Must make sure she doesn't get too drunk, if she does I'll talk to her friend, the black one, what's her name again? Doesn't matter. I'll talk to her and say something like: 'Hey, do you think Amy's OK? I just don't know if he should be acting like that if she's drunk.' With any luck they'll label him a "creep" and he'll be finished. Door's open, good. Piss first then see about the sabotage.

'Hey! Just heading to the bathroom one sec,'

'Just going to the bathroom,'

'Hey man! Just going to the bathroom I'll be right back.'

This is exhausting. And it's so hot in here I'm sweating. How come some people never seem to sweat? It's not fair. Oh that feels good I needed that. How many drinks now seven or eight? If I keep this up the night'll get ugly. Fuck that was good. I wonder if he has any deodorant in the medicine cabinet, I don't stand a chance without it. Hey, what's this?

'Mi-no-xi..? Jesus Christ!'

Got you you prick! I knew there had to be something. Acting like some bon vivant, all the while slathering this shit on his head! This is fucking excellent, this is the best thing that could have happened! But how can you use it? There must be a way. That's it! I know exactly what I'll do! It's so simple. Just leave it out like that, perfect, anyone could've done it. Have I got some of that coke left? A bit, good, thank God. Where's Amy?

'Sorry guys coming through,

'Have you guys seen Amy? Kitchen?

'Coming through guys sorry going to the kitchen.'

There she is. And she's alone! I don't have wine on my lips do I? That happened last time and I looked like a prick. No I think I'm alright. OK here goes.

'Hey, how's it going?'

'Oh hey! Good it's great here everyone's so nice!'

'Yeah they are aren't they?'

'And *he* is so nice! I can't believe I've never met him before. He knows so much about Africa.'

Fucking bastard.

'Yeah he's an awesome guy, really awesome. Hey Amy, listen. I've got some coke left and I was wondering if you'd like to-'

'-Sure.'

'Really? Great. Bathroom?'

'Yeah let's do it!'

And we're off! I should be a fucking general or something. Yeah that's right you pricks, get a good look, we're going to the bathroom together. Sure it's just for the coke right now, but who knows what might happen? Just need to ruin this bastard first.

'Wow that is *good.*'

'Yeah I got it from a friend of mine in London.'

'Awesome, you should introduce me sometime.'

Not fucking likely.

'Hey, wait a minute. What's this?'

'What?'

'This? OMG! I know what this is!'

'What, what is it?'

'*Oh my God*! I'm going to tell the girls.'

Victory. Total victory.

'Thanks so much by the way you're really sweet. See you later on?'

'No problem! Definitely.'

And goodbye Mr. IR. Fucking prick.

so what do you think about gaza?

'So what do you think about Gaza?'

'Huh?'

'Gaza. Like, what do you think about Gaza?'

Wake up idiot, she's said something. Need to tread carefully. Where is she from? I really should've listened when I asked her. She is pretty dark, maybe she's an Arab. What was her name again? Sara? Could be an Arab name. But the Israelis are pretty dark too aren't they? And there's that hummus named Sara, or is that Sabra? This is really too much. This is high stakes stuff. This is my life here.

'I think its awful.'

Risky move. Maybe she'll give you a clue.

'What's awful?'

Who is this girl? Who asks something like that? Why is she torturing me like this?

'Just all the people dying. All the innocent people.'

'Yeah. But who's innocent?'

Jesus Christ. Who is this girl? She must be a politics student. Did she say she studied politics? Or was it photography? What the fuck am I going to say?

'What do you think?'

Brilliant. You might actually be a genius.

'You first I asked first.'

Fuck. She's getting suspicious. If I get this wrong I'm finished, she'll call me a Zionist pig or a Nazi pig and this dinner will've been for nothing. I need to say something. Fucking anything. Move your mouth.

'Who's innocent? That's an interesting question. Of course the Israelis have done some bad things, but so have the Palestinians. And you know, people talk about civilians and stuff but really even they're not innocent. Nobody's innocent really. We've all got our own demons, our own hatreds and prejudices, and I think it's important to recognise that.'

Is this working? God I wish she'd do something. Give me a sign. Better keep going.

'And you know it can't just be saying things, we have to do things as well to recognise that, you know what I mean? Like, it's no use just saying you hate things and you're not innocent unless you prove it by trying not to hate things. It's all about the trying I think.'

'Wow.'

Oh God here it comes. She's going to shit all over me. She'll probably tell everyone, put it on the university confessions page, my God I'm fucked.

'I can tell you're like super well read.'

Lord in Heaven.

'Do you read a lot about this sort of stuff?'

'Oh. A little bit here and there. What about you?'

'Huh?'

'What side's innocent?'

'Oh! Aha. I don't really know to be honest I was just asking!'

She's a photography student then. My cup runneth over.

POEMS

the wall

'Doors are unopened, words are unspoken;

No one smiles as once they did.

Young men avoid her, and women whisper,

She's no chance now for a kid.

She's had her career, has given it years,

Clawing her way to the boardroom,

But turning her thoughts to weddings and tots,

Finds, in pursuit of a bridegroom,

In spite of her desk and all her success,

No matter how desperate her bid,

That Tony wants Tess, and Jamie's with Jess,

And women her age are just "mid".

She's now getting fat, surrounded by cats,

With decades of work yet to come,

Pining for brats from a one bedroom flat,

And drinking until she goes numb.

windrush elegy

We dun bin comin on dah boat,

From islinds in dah watah sea,

An' wen dah boat come stop to float

We dun bin heah, as you can see.

Dah place is big, dah people's big,

Dey dun been bildin out ah stone.

We dun come heah, an' git a gig,

Buh Lord! Dey work man han' to bone!

Dah wimin heah don't like me much,

Dey scream an' scoul when black man come;

Dey 'bigated' to me an' such,

All cause me like to drink me rum!

In oldin' place dah sun was bright,

Wit many fruits all on dah trees,

Buh heah dah groun' gan cold an' white,

An' everytin dun cost a piece!

abdul kareem

In the year two thousand one hundred and twenty-eight, ,

I'll reincarnate on the Grasmere social housing estate.

I'll go to work in the programming pod, and inspect

The plaque above our shack where some old poet's house once stood,

And dine on crickets redeemed with tickets,

Distributed by local hub officer Shaqbool Mahmood.

But when I dream, I, citizen Abdul Kareem,

Will sweat at the sight of an old oak tree,

And remember the man I used to be.

looksmaxxing

The disgusting health of youth

Is what I'm jealous of.

The easy sleep, the hard-ons proof,

Even after hours of getting off;

The glow and the thick hair

On smooth and moleless shoulders;

The few, fast-wasted years

It's not absurd to be lovers.

No use trying to get it back;

Did Narcissus microneedle?

Better to wait until it all goes black,

And pray you're not reborn a beetle.

tourists

Men with upturned polo collars,

Fat little families in tow,

Aimlessly spend all their dollars

On magnets, pizzas to-go

And shoddy plastic Davids.

With such mammals waddling there,

Who can breathe the Tuscan air?

'But the economy!' Save it.

I'd rather millions starving, really,

Circled by ravening vultures,

Than fatties in the Loggia dei Lanzi,

Who think they can eat all cultures.

mortality

I think of weddings, birthdays, workdays,

Weekends and holidays;

How all of them tend to the same sorry end;

How nothing we do can overcome you,

Death,

My punctual friend.

sundays

Sometimes, on Sundays, I'll go in,

Sit at the back and watch,

Past creaking pews, cold to the touch,

The little service begin.

The priest, the schoolboys, dressed in white,

Out of the vestry come,

The air at once grows thick, and light

From the windows settles down

On Filipinos with guitars.

I stay and watch it all. What to tell?

Need I describe the sermon, the bell,

The shambling waferwards,

The scattered way they cough and sing?

No point; I've nothing to declare.

But I find I like my being there,

In spite of the thing.

waiting tables

The rich, in subtly better clothes;

Their large and confident progeny;

My masters, really, I suppose;

Gods of the service economy.

Oh, they smile, smile all night long,

Ordering old, expensive drinks,

Smile even if something's wrong,

Correcting you, as glasses clink,

And all the while you can think

Of nothing else but what you'd give

To have a pair of silver links

And a tailored shirt, like his.

apparuit

She wears a dress,

Without success,

Bought some years ago,

And every eye

That passes by,

Drops and dies like snow.

traffic

Engines hum and sirens blare

A passage to their labours,

Quick to merge and quick to sever,

Stopping, starting, there.

break-up

She has acted appropriately.

Her friends assure her she has.

For me,

I can't but hate how quickly, quietly

Affections pass.

grasmere

I feel like a fly on a looking-glass.

A single spot the light can't pass.

stood up

His hair is parted and combed.

His shirt is tucked in and pressed.

Clearly, he is waiting for someone.

Twenty minutes,

Thirty go by.

He sighs,

And looks relieved.

liberation

Commuting, with a chai latte,

A copy of Plath in her tote,

She opens a slightly battered MacBook,

Covered in Post-it notes.

Hills roll by, quick-covered, unseen;

The ads are all in Comic Sans;

There's a crack in her iPhone's screen;

At home she's doing an OnlyFans.

politics

Well, the Arabs, I suppose -

I'm not so much attached;

My politics are only those

Of her with whom I've matched.

She's a red? Then I'm a red;

She's a Tory? Tory.

So long as we end up in bed,

I'll tell her any story.

tren

You might have money,

You might have hair,

You might have spent a year on tren.

It doesn't matter

In the slightest,

If you're only five foot ten.

epigrams

I

She is twenty-five next month.

On that day I shall wear black.

II

'Sex work?'

With you it would be, I suppose.

III

She sees a man at six o'clock,

The seventh man this year,

And brings him home at ten o'clock,

And might see him next year.

IV

A nose ring?

I always knew you were a cow.

V

Does the adjective 'alive,'

Hold any force past twenty-five?

From what I've seen, it seems to be,

That most are dead by twenty-three.

VI

The sleepless gooner,

Watching the sun mount skyward,

Closes the curtains.

VII

Terminal exposure to X,

And for fourteen months, no sex.

A steady coarsening of the soul,

Turning his heart into coal.

Printed in Great Britain
by Amazon